E
POM

LAKESIDE JOINT SCHOOL DISTRICT

19621 BLACK ROAD

LOS GATOS, CALIFORNIA 95030

TELEPHONE (408) 354-2372

POSY

BY **CHARLOTTE POMERANTZ**
PICTURES BY
CATHERINE STOCK

GREENWILLOW BOOKS NEW YORK

FOR RUTH AND DAVID
—C. P.

FOR DARIA AND GREG
—C. S.

Library of Congress Cataloging in Publication Data
Pomerantz, Charlotte.   Posy.
Summary: Posy and her father reminisce about the things
she used to do when she was a very little girl.
[1. Fathers and daughters — Fiction]
I. Stock, Catherine, ill.   II. Title.
PZ7.P77Po 1983   [E]   83-1452
ISBN 0-688-02298-7   ISBN 0-688-02299-5 (lib. bdg.)

CONTENTS

"Daddy," said Posy, "tell me
a story about me. About when
I was little."
So Daddy told her a story.

POSY AND THE SHEETS

One day, when you were little, Mommy and I decided that we needed some new sheets. The sheets we had were old and full of holes and patches. So I told Mommy I would call up the store and order new ones.

"Good," said Mommy. "Then I can go to
the fish market."
She put on her coat, picked up her
pocketbook, and walked toward the door.
"What kind of sheets should I order?"
I asked her.
"Any kind," said Mommy. "We need four
pairs."
"Shall I get them plain or with a design?"
"I don't care," she said.
"But what color do you like?" I asked her.
"Any color," she said. She kissed me and
walked out the door.

That's when you looked up at me and said PINK. You didn't know many words, but one of them was pink.

"Stay with me, Po," I said to you. "I need your help."

9

I called up the store and told the saleswoman that I wanted to order some
sheets.

"What color?" she asked.

"Pink," I said.

"Do you want them in plain pink or pink
with pink stripes?"

I asked her to hold on. "Po," I said, "do
you want them in plain pink or pink
with pink stripes?"

PINK, you said.

I told the saleswoman, "I'd like one pair
of plain pink sheets and one pair of pink
sheets with pink stripes."

"Will that be all?" the saleswoman asked.

"No," I said. "I need two more pairs."

"Let's see," she said. "We have sheets with flowers and sheets with fish. They come in all colors."

"One moment," I said. "Po, they have sheets with flowers and sheets with fish. They come in lots of colors. What should I get?"

PINK, you said.

"Hello," I said to the saleswoman, "I want one pair of sheets with pink flowers, and one pair of sheets with pink fish."

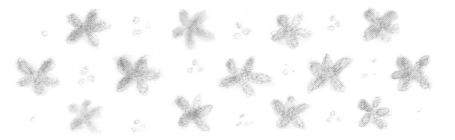

The saleswoman said, "I will repeat your order to make sure it is right:

1 pair of plain pink sheets,

1 pair of pink sheets with pink stripes,

1 pair of sheets with pink flowers,

1 pair of sheets with pink fish."

"That is correct," I said.

14

"Thank you for your order," said the saleswoman.

Then she said, "Are you sure you want all the sheets in pink?"

"Wait a minute," I said. "I'll check."

I turned to you. "Po," I said, "are you sure you want all the sheets in pink?"

PINK, you said.

Posy chuckled. "So that's why all our sheets are pink."

"Yes," said Daddy. "Do you like them?"

"No," said Posy. "I hate pink."

"Daddy," said Posy, "tell me
another story."
"No," said Daddy. "It's bedtime."
"One more," said Posy.
So Daddy told her another story.

POSY AND THE NIGHTTIME

One day, when you were little, you said, "Daddy, I have been thinking and thinking. Where do you and Mommy go when you go out at night?"
So I told you, "We visit friends. Or we go out to dinner in a restaurant, and afterwards we go to a movie or a concert."

You said, "Do you have a nice time?"

And I said, "Very nice."

You said, "And then what?"

"We come home and we go to your room."

"Am I asleep?" you asked.

"Yes. You are fast asleep. Sometimes you have kicked off the covers. We put the sheet back over you. And then the blanket. And in wintertime another blanket."

"Do I wake up?" you asked.

"No. You go on sleeping."

"Where is my lion?" you asked.

"Sometimes it is next to you and
   sometimes it has fallen to the floor.
   If it is on the floor, we pick it up
   and put it next to you."

"And after that?" you asked.

"After that, we kiss you good night."

"Why," you asked.

"Because we love you."

"Do you always do that?"

"Always."

   But that was not the end.

The next night, at bedtime, you smiled
and said, "Now I know what you do when
you go out at night. You have a nice
time. And then you come home.
You cover me with a sheet. And then a
blanket. And sometimes another blanket.
If my lion is on the floor, you put it
next to me. You kiss me and I don't
wake up because I am asleep."

"I said all that!" said Posy.

"You did. And then you asked again,
'Do you always kiss me?'"

"To make sure," said Posy.

"Yes," said Daddy. "And I said <u>always</u>."
Daddy winked at Posy. "And do you
know what?"

Posy nodded. "I know," she said. "You
still do."

"Daddy," said Posy, "tell me one more
  story about me."
"I've already told you two," said Daddy.
"Just one more," said Posy. "I like stories
  in threes."

POSY AND THE POCKETBOOK

When you were little, Mommy gave you her old pocketbook. I put in three dimes.

"Is this enough to buy a chocolate bar?" you asked.

"Yes," I said. "You can buy a chocolate bar for twenty-five cents and get back a nickel in change."

Of course that was ages ago. Nowadays, chocolate bars cost much more. You were very excited. Your first pocketbook. Your first real money. You didn't stop talking all the way to the store.

You said, "When I get there, I'm going to go right up to the man. I'll say, Excuse me, man. I want to buy a chocolate bar.

The man will say, which one do you want, miss?

I will point to it and then I will take my money out of my pocketbook. Here, man, I will say, here is the money.

He'll give me the chocolate bar and say, Here is your change. Then he will notice my pocketbook. My, he will say, what a grown-up pocketbook! Have a good day and thank you.

And I'll say, Thank <u>you</u>."

But as soon as you stepped inside the
store, you stopped talking.
The man said, "May I help you, miss?"
But you just stared at the floor and
didn't say a word.

Finally, I picked out a chocolate bar for you and told you to pay for it. You opened your pocketbook.

But when you took out the three dimes, they slipped through your fingers and fell between the candy bars.

The man moved the candy around and tried to find the money. But he couldn't.

"That's all right," he said.

"I'll find it later. Here is a nickel change, anyway."

As we left the store, the man said, "Have a nice day and thank you."

"Say <u>thank you</u>, Posy," I said.

You tried, but your voice was so tiny and scared that I don't think he heard you.

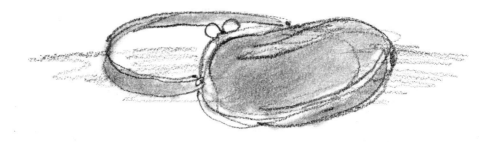

Daddy put his arms around Posy.

"Do you remember that day ages ago?"

"Yes," said Posy. "I never forgot it."

"Good night, Posy."

"Good night, Daddy. Daddy?"

"No," said Daddy. "No more stories."

39

"I don't want you to tell me another story,"
said Posy. "I just want to know the name
if you were going to tell me one."

"Good night, Posy."

"Just the name, Daddy."

Daddy sighed and scratched his ear.

"The name is POSY AND THE WISHES."

"Wishes?" said Posy. "What sort of wishes?"

"Wishes you used to wish when you were
little. Good night."

Daddy walked toward the door.

Posy began to recite:

 "Star light, star bright,

  First star I see tonight,

  I wish I may, I wish I might,

  Have the wish I wish tonight."

Daddy's face lit up. He turned around.

"You remember!" he said.

"Of course," said Posy.

"My," he said. "And do you remember the wishing game we used to play on summer nights in the country?"

Posy lay back on her pillow.

"Remind me," she said.

"I recited the poem," said Daddy, "and you looked out the window and picked a star to wish on. Sometimes you wished you could catch a butterfly. Or a fish. Or a yellow rabbit.

Once you wished you were a plumber, so you could fix the toilet.

When there were no stars or when it was raining, you wished on a raindrop. One rainy night, you wished you were a candy man in a candy store selling candy.

Then one night, a few days before we came home to the city, you said, 'I wish I could be a grown-up lady. I wish I could take an airplane tomorrow night with my grandpa.

And I want two more wishes. I wish I had three grandmas and a hundred balloons.'"

"Wow," said Posy. "So many wishes!
What did I wish for the next night?"
"Nothing," said Daddy. "You didn't want to
play the wishing game anymore. I think
you were all wished out. Do you
remember?"
"Of course," said Posy. "I just needed to
be reminded."